DEAR BABY

Tammy Le

AuthorHouse™
1663 Liberty Drive
Bloomington, IN 47403
www.authorhouse.com
Phone: 1 (800) 839-8640

Published by AuthorHouse 05/14/2019

ISBN: 978-1-7283-1205-7 (sc)
ISBN: 978-1-7283-1206-4 (e)

Print information available on the last page.

authorHOUSE®

You need to help out
and clean your own room,
Because mommy gave you life
from inside her womb.

And even though you were very tiny
and didn't weigh a ton,
We still cradled you in our arms
until you were one.

And even though milk was expensive,
we still knew...
We had to bottle feed you
until you were two.

And even though your diapers were smelly,
You will see...
We had to change your diapers
until you were three.

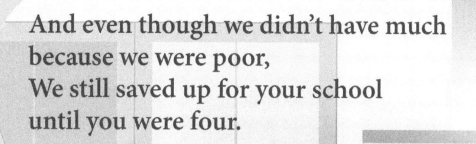

And even though we didn't have much
because we were poor,
We still saved up for your school
until you were four.

And even though you are
healthy and alive,
We still struggled everyday
until you were five.

And even though
you drive us a little insane,
Our love for you
will never change

Do you remember
when you were sick in bed?
We made you feel better
and kissed your head

And when you wanted to learn
all the things you like
We taught you how to ride
your very first bike

So even though we
didn't get much sleep,
We still worked hard
for everything you reap

ABOUT THE AUTHOR

Tammy Le

Fortunate enough to grow up in beautiful Calgary Alberta thanks to my refugee parents that escaped Vietnam and came to Canada to give birth to me. My parents came to a foreign country not speaking a word of English and with absolutely nothing in their pocket. I grew up very poor having two younger brothers, we never knew the meaning of poor nor did we know how much our parents struggled until we were much older. What pains me the most is knowing that I was an entitled little kid that always gave my parents a hard time if I didn't get what I want. I never fully appreciated everything they did for me until I had my first child. I knew I couldn't possibly be the only kid out there that caused havoc upon their parents but I knew it was so wrong. It shouldn't take kids these days this long to understand appreciation so I wrote this book thinking of my parents and in hopes of sending out a message to kids all around the world. I just want every parent out there to not go unappreciated.

I love writing educational children's books with meaning behind them so if you enjoyed this book you may want to check out my other books!

CPSIA information can be obtained
at www.ICGtesting.com
Printed in the USA
BVHW051724270519
549348BV00027B/2718